To all children, learn to love to learn, explore and create!
-Ashley H. A. Williams

Written & Illustrated By: Ashley H.A. Williams *Copyright © 2015*

All right reserved. Published in the United States by Ashley H. A. Williams, Virginia.

Visit our website:

MILK & HONEY BOOKS
www.MilkandHoneyBooks.com

ISSN 2376-0591

Happy Hands Learn to Count Book

Written & Illustrated By:
Ashley H.A. Williams

ONE

1

ONE

There is 1 world.

TWO

2

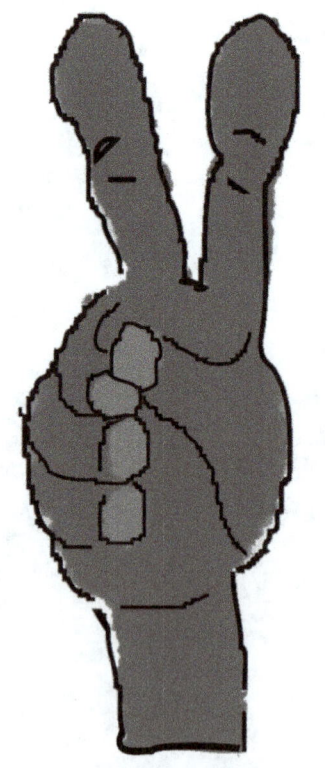

TWO
2

You and Mr. Beans have something's alike.

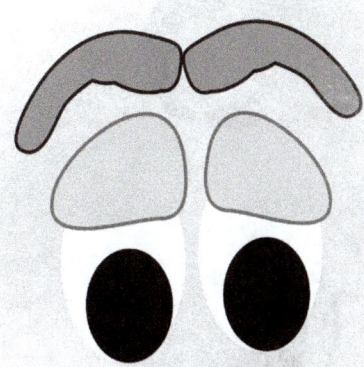

Mr. Beans has two eyes just like you.
To see everything.

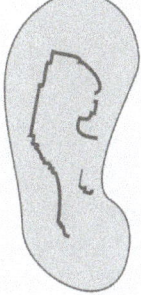

Mr. Beans has two ears just like you.
To hear everything.

Mr. Beans has two teeth just like you.
To eat everything.

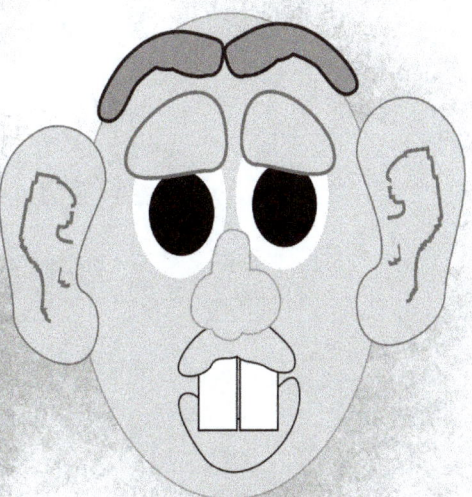

Mr. Beans is cool just like you..

THREE

3

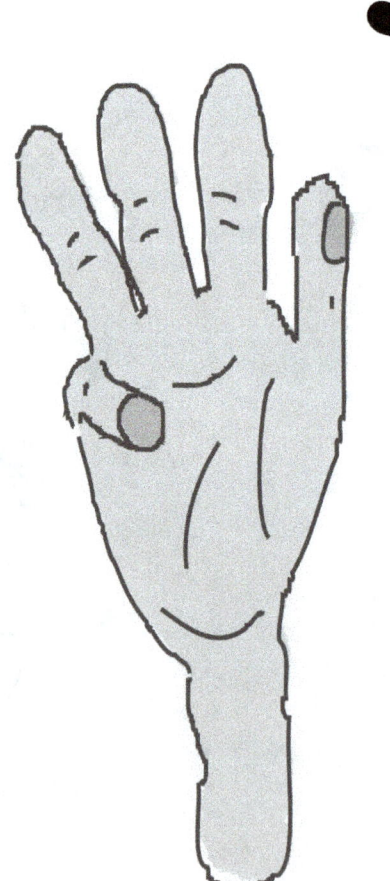

THREE

Nacho Man has  sides, like a triangle.

I am no Taco.
I am Nacho, Nacho Man.

FOUR

4

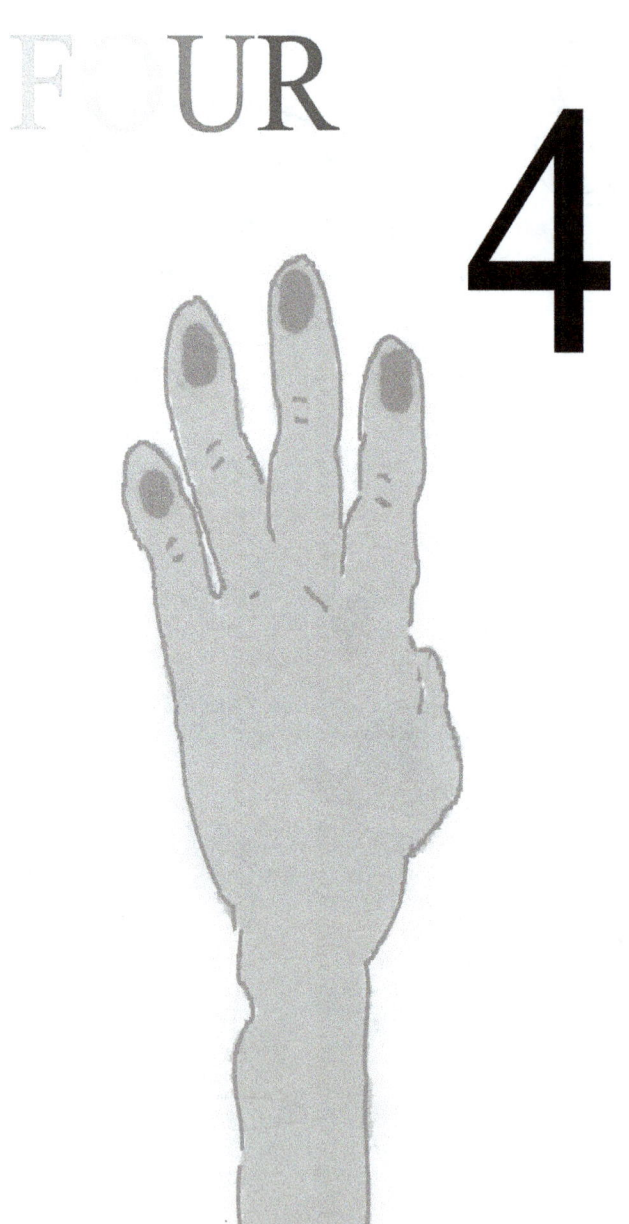

FOUR

There are **4** seasons in a year.

Spring is when plants grow.

Summer is when the Sun shines hard all day.

Spring is when the leafs fall from the Tree's.

Winter is very cold and snow falls.

FIVE

5

There are **5** points on a Star.

You are like a Star so shine!

SIX

6

SIX

There are **6** buttons on Judy's coat.

There are **6** buttons on Judy's umbrella.

Now Judy is ready to play!

SEVEN

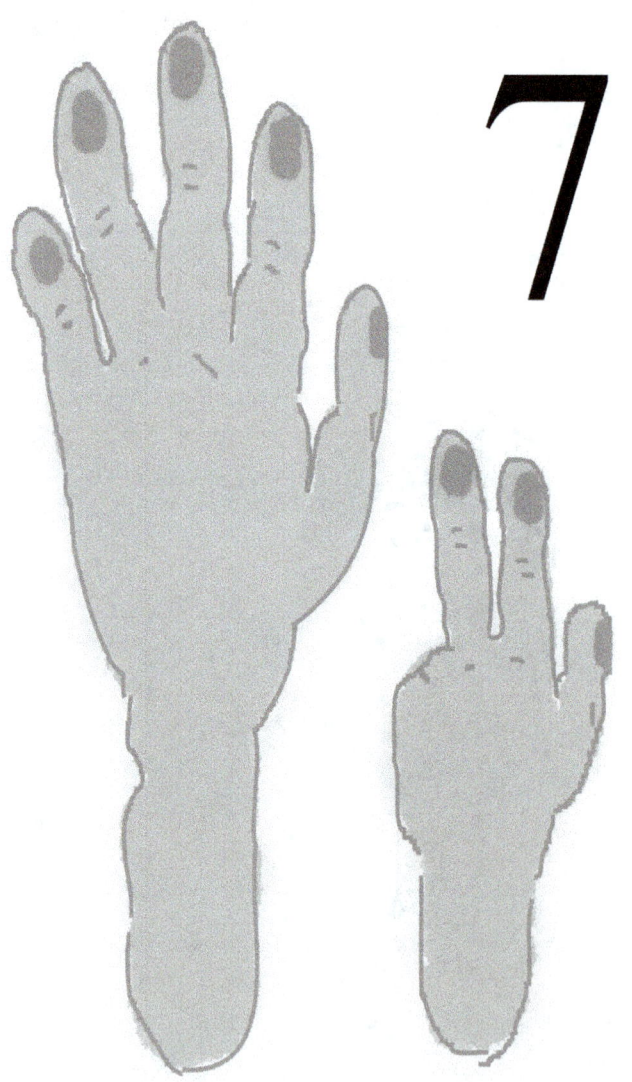

7

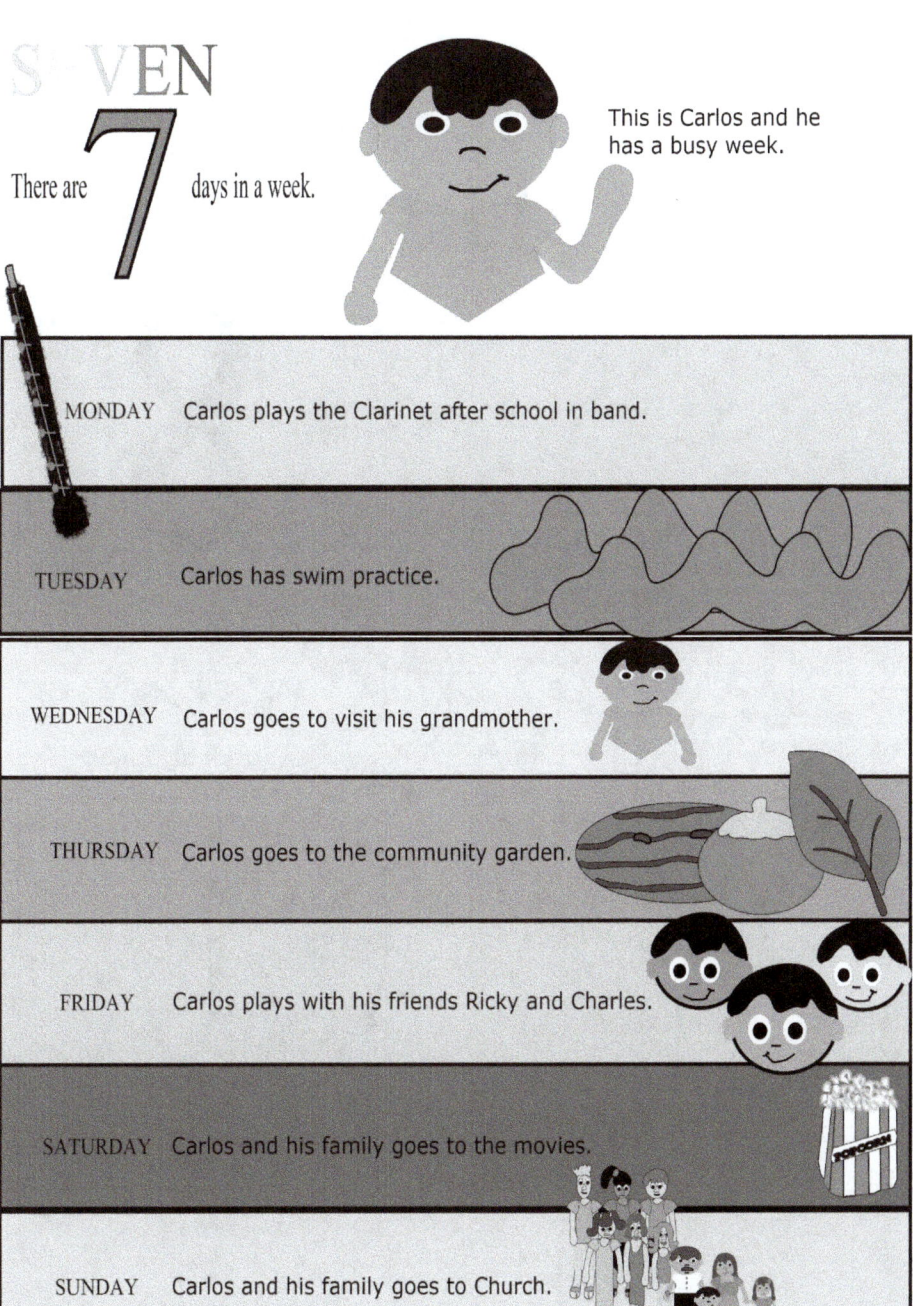

SEVEN

7

There are **7** days in a week.

This is Carlos and he has a busy week.

MONDAY	Carlos plays the Clarinet after school in band.
TUESDAY	Carlos has swim practice.
WEDNESDAY	Carlos goes to visit his grandmother.
THURSDAY	Carlos goes to the community garden.
FRIDAY	Carlos plays with his friends Ricky and Charles.
SATURDAY	Carlos and his family goes to the movies.
SUNDAY	Carlos and his family goes to Church.

EIGHT

8

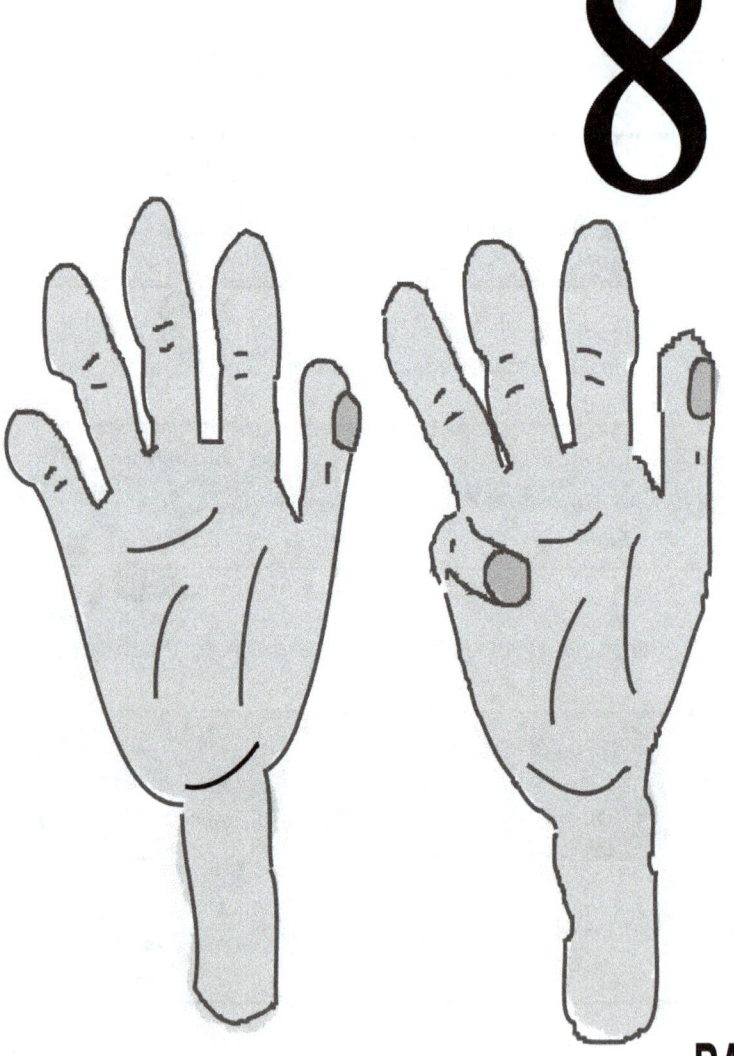

EIGHT

There are **8** legs on Ollie the Octopus.

Ollie the Octopus loves Crabs.

NINE

9

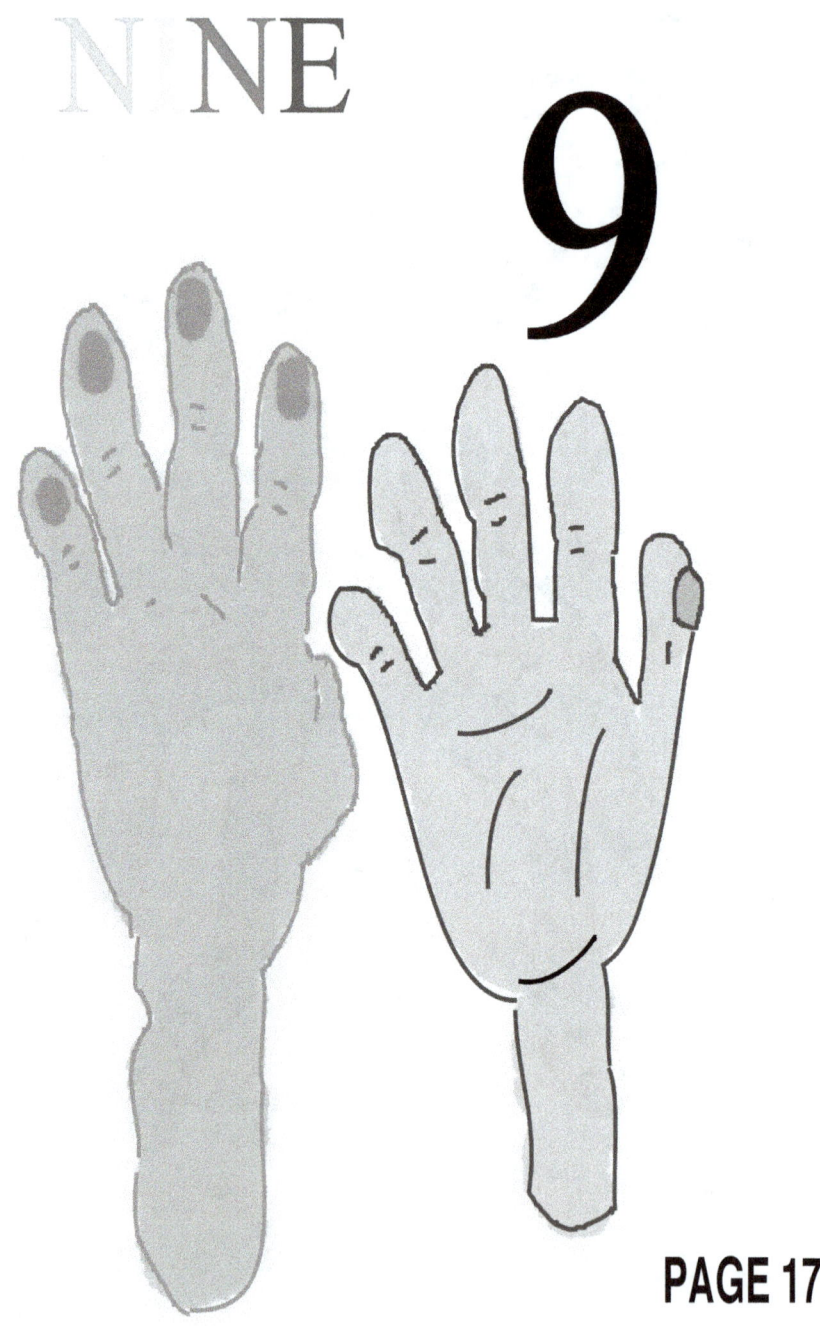

NINE

9 Fruits and Veggies will make you strong like a superhero.

TEN 10

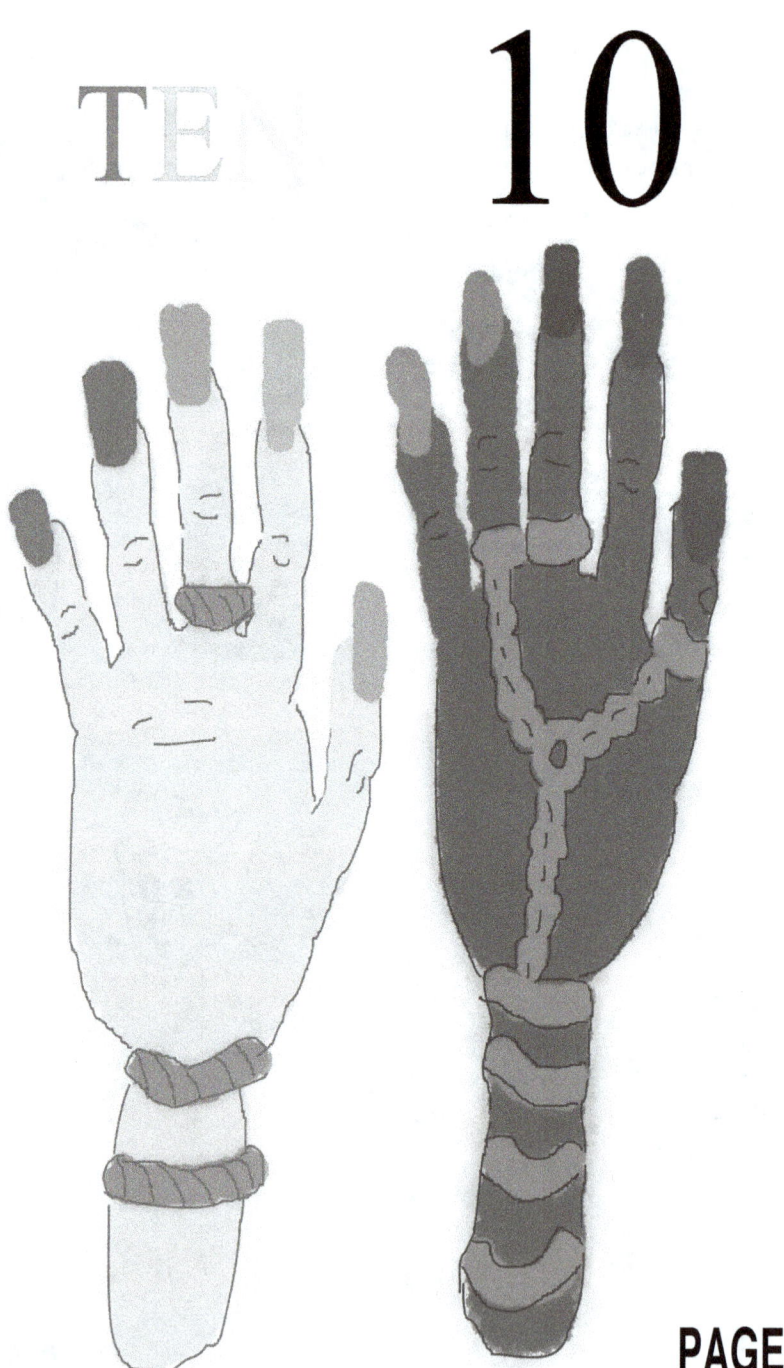

Teeny tiny Tim the train picks up 10 bags of mail everyday.

Teeny tiny Tim the train takes all the mail to everyone in Trainsville.

www.ingramcontent.com/pod-product-compliance
Lightning Source LLC
Chambersburg PA
CBHW060957120626
46557CB00003B/1200